and the Terrible Dragon

THE JOLLY JESTER

The king and queen of Busylande lived in a big castle
with the knights and ladies of the court. The king's
pride and joy was his little daughter, Princess Lily.
Sometimes the happy princess danced for the members
of the court while they waited for the royal dinner.

Here comes the castle cook, Big Hilda,
with the king's soup. Be careful, Big Hilda!

The peasants of Busylande lived and
worked in the fields around the castle.

One of the friendliest and best workers
was named Peasant Pig.

Peasant Pig always waved to
Princess Lily when he saw her
riding outside the castle
in her royal wagon.

After the peasants cut and threshed the wheat, they took the grain to the miller, who ground it into flour.

Baker Fox made delicious bread from the flour.

At harvest time, the peasants picked grapes and put them into a big vat. They squashed the grapes with their feet to make grape juice.

Squish! Squash! You're doing a good job, Lowly Worm!

One day, the king declared a holiday in Busylande.
Everyone went into the fields outside the castle to
play games and celebrate. The knights on their horses
played a game of jousting. They tried to knock each
other off their horses. Oh my! Jousting is a rough game!
The peasants wrestled . . . and played ball.

They danced and sang and drank
lots of grape juice. Everyone had fun.

Look at that juggler juggling plates!

Peasant Pig practiced
with his lance. He
wanted very much
to become a knight.

Watch out, Peasant Pig!
That make-believe knight
can fight back. . . .

Peasant Pig hit the target, but the make-believe knight spun around and hit him back.

You forgot to duck, Peasant Pig. You need more practice before you can become a knight.

Then Peasant Pig and Lowly Worm tried the game of quoits. Lowly tossed *himself*—and won!

But Peasant Pig won the archery contest. He shot the apple off the tree stump with his bow and arrow.

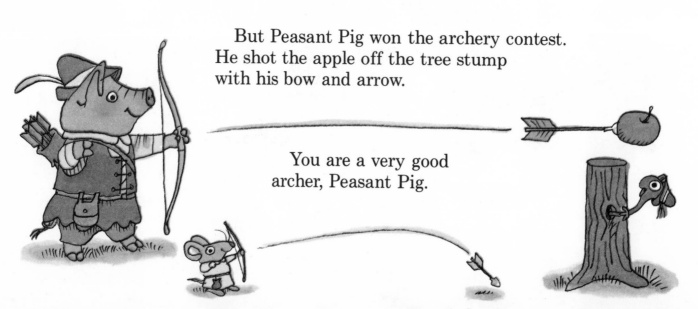

You are a very good archer, Peasant Pig.

Suddenly everyone heard a cry for help.
It came from the woods. "What is happening?"
the crowd asked. Peasant Pig used Lowly as
an arrow and shot him high into the air.

"What do you see?" asked Peasant Pig.

"A DRAGON!" Lowly shouted. "Run,
everybody! Run for your lives!"

Everyone ran to the castle.
The king, the queen, the
knights, the ladies, and
the peasants all crossed the
drawbridge into the big,
safe castle.

The guards quickly cranked up
the drawbridge. Peasant Pig made
it just in time! Now the dragon would
have a hard time getting into the castle.

Everyone was safe inside the walls of the castle—
except Princess Lily. She had not come back from her
ride in the country.

"Find her!" roared the king.

"Save my baby!" sobbed the queen.

Peasant Pig wanted to help the king and queen. "I will
go to the lookout tower," said Peasant Pig.

But Peasant Pig and Lowly
could not see the princess.
"Lowly, I need your help
again," said Peasant Pig.

He shot Lowly into the air.
"What do you see, Lowly?" asked Peasant Pig.
"I see the princess!" Lowly shouted. "The dragon has tied up the guards and captured her!"

When Peasant Pig told the king
what Lowly had seen, the king
flew into a rage.

"I'll show that dragon!" he shouted.
"Call my knights. They must slay the
dragon and rescue my little Lily."

Peasant Pig wished
he were a knight.
He wanted to go, too.

The knights rushed to put on their
armor to fight the terrible dragon.

The armor was so heavy that Peasant Pig
had to help the knights get onto their horses.
"Thank you, Peasant Pig," said the knights.

In the forest, poor Princess Lily was now a prisoner. The dragon had tied her up and put her to work making grape juice.

The royal guards could not help Princess Lily.

But help was on its way! The king's knights
rode out of the castle, crossed the drawbridge
over the moat, and galloped into the forest.
The brave knights charged . . .

But the terrible dragon leaped up!
The horses were scared. They
stopped in their tracks so suddenly
that the knights were thrown out
of their saddles.

Klunk! Klunk! Klunk! Klunk!

The knights lay on their backs. Their armor was so
heavy, they could not get up. The dragon laughed at them.
Oh, that terrible dragon!

But look! It was not a real dragon! It was a band of
robbers dressed up like a dragon. When they saw that
the knights couldn't get up, the robbers took off
their dragon costume.

Then the robbers tied up the knights and
dressed themselves in the knights' armor.
Now they thought *they* were brave knights.
Oh, those awful fellows!

Princess Lily watched as Morbert, the leader
of the robbers, shot an arrow toward the castle.

The arrow flew over the head of the king. Lowly saw that a piece of paper was tied to it.

The arrow flew into the kitchen and landed right in the middle of Big Hilda's freshly baked cake. SPLAT! Big Hilda was FURIOUS.

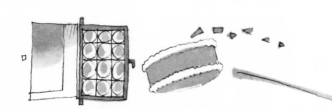

"Someone has ruined my beautiful cake!" she cried. She was so angry, she threw the cake out the window.
Lowly hurried in to find the note that was tied to the arrow.

In the forest, the robbers were sitting down
and drinking grape juice. Suddenly they had
Big Hilda's cake to go with their juice.

At the castle, Peasant Pig and Lowly brought the
robbers' note to the king. It said, "Give us all your
gold and jewels, and you can have your daughter back
safe and sound. Signed, Morbert and his terrible dragon."
The king was frightened. He rushed to his
counting house to get his gold and precious jewels.

Peasant Pig decided to try to save Princess Lily himself. "I have an idea," he said to Lowly, "but I will need a lot of soap to make it work."

Big Hilda brought Peasant Pig all the bars of soap in the castle. Peasant Pig filled up the throwing machine with the soap and climbed in. Lowly cranked up the machine.

KITCHEN

SOAP

Aim carefully, Lowly.

Good shot, Lowly!

Peasant Pig and all of the soap landed right in the grape juicer where Princess Lily was squashing the grapes.

Splash. Splosh.

Burrble. Burrble.

The grape juice began to turn into grape soap-suds.

You'd better pay attention, robbers.

"Ah! Now the grape juice is
nice and bubbly!" said Morbert.

Morbert, Merbert, Orgbert, Ergbert, and
Sherbert took big gulps of the grape soap-suds.
"UGGH!" they cried. "Water! We need WATER!"

What's the matter, robbers?
Don't you like Peasant Pig's
grape soap-suds?

"There's water in the moat," said Morbert. All the
robbers jumped into the moat to get a big drink of water.

"Ahhh," said Morbert, after he rinsed the grape soap-suds out of his mouth. "That is much better."

Then he and the other robbers tried to climb out of the moat. But their armor was too heavy.

"We are trapped!" they cried.

"That looks like Morbert and his gang," said the king.

Big Hilda wanted to see
the robbers, too.
Look out, Big Hilda!
Don't lean over too far!

Uh-oh! Big Hilda
didn't listen.

Big Hilda landed with a BIG splash.
She splashed the robbers right out of the moat.

"Look, the robbers are coming back,"
said Peasant Pig. "Quick, Princess
Lily, where is the dragon?"

"There is no dragon," she answered.
"The robbers used a dragon *costume*.
It is in the woods."

"Aha!" said Peasant Pig. "Now I know what to do. Wait here. Don't worry!" He leaped out of the grape juicer.

He untied the knights and the guards.
"Hurry!" Peasant Pig said to them.
"Follow me. It's our turn to be a dragon."

When the robbers reached the forest,
Peasant Pig Dragon jumped out at them!

"A DRAGON!" shrieked Morbert, Merbert,
Orgbert, Ergbert, and Sherbert. It was
their turn to be frightened.

Klink! Klank! Klunk!
The robbers dressed in heavy armor
fell to the ground. They couldn't move.

Peasant Pig quickly tied them up.

Then he untied Princess Lily.
"I'll give you a Peasant-Pig-Dragon ride home," he said.

Princess Lily laughed and jumped on the dragon's back.

When the king saw the
dragon with his daughter, he
was very upset. He didn't know
it was Peasant Pig Dragon.

Big Hilda thought the
dragon was real, too.
"Help! Help!" she called.
"Lower the drawbridge and let me in!"

But Lowly had an idea. He said to the king, "I know
how to stop a dragon. All I need is a lot of pepper."
The king ran to the kitchen and took a sack of pepper.

"Tie it around my neck,"
said Lowly. "Now I need
Sheriff Murphy's help."

Then Lowly told Sheriff
Murphy to shoot him at the
dragon with his crossbow.
You're a good arrow, Lowly.

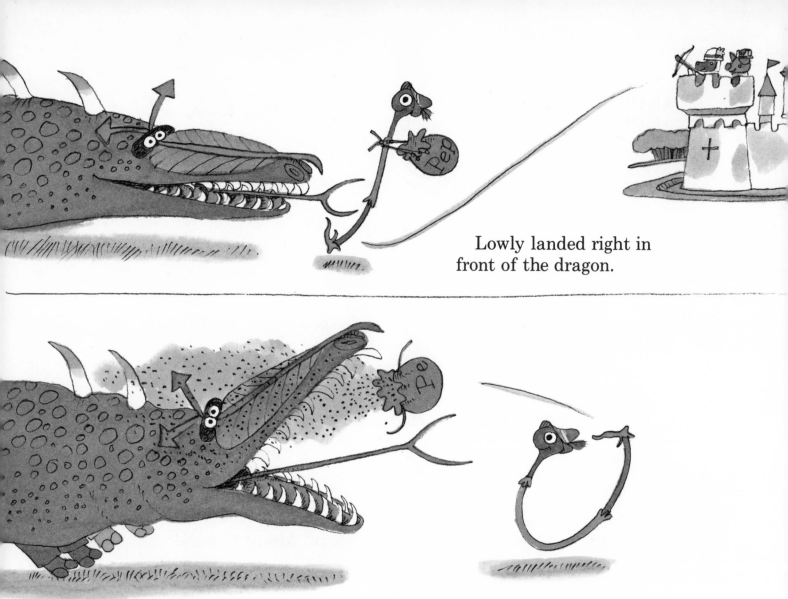

Lowly landed right in
front of the dragon.

He tossed the whole sack of
pepper into the dragon's mouth.

"Ah-CHOO!" sneezed the dragon.

"Ah-CHOO!" sneezed Peasant Pig.
"Ah-CHOO!" sneezed Princess Lily.
"Ah-CHOO!" sneezed the knights and guards.
Everyone tumbled out of the dragon costume.
"Hi, Lowly," said Peasant Pig.

Princess Lily gave Peasant Pig a big kiss.
"How can we ever thank you?" she asked him.

"I know how," said the king. "Kneel, Peasant Pig."
He touched Peasant Pig on the shoulder with
his royal sword.

"I name you Sir Peasant Pig, the bravest knight in
the kingdom." Then he gave Sir Peasant Pig a shiny
new suit of armor.

"And, Lowly," said the king, "because you are
such a funny fellow, I name you my court jester." Then
he gave Lowly the best jester suit ever.

Everyone was happy, including the queen. She was
so happy, she was crying!

As for the robbers, they were sent
to the castle dungeon. There they
were put to work making soap.

They won't be playing dragon again
for a long time!

"We must celebrate!" said the king.
"Yes! Yes!" everyone shouted.
They all sat down at the king's table
for a feast.
To amuse the king, Lowly the jolly
jester tried his new juggling act—
with fresh eggs!
You need more practice, Lowly!
Everyone laughed and had a good time.

Lowly took the eggs
that weren't broken back
to the kitchen.

Big Hilda had just finished baking
a beautiful new cake. She brought it
to the table.

The king was about to cut the cake
when—out jumped a little dragon!
Everyone was very surprised. Then the
dragon stuck out its tongue and—
guess what?

It was a Lowly Worm Dragon!
What a funny fellow!
The royal friends all sat down
again. And, from that day on,
everyone in the kingdom of Busylande
lived a very good and happy life.